NEW YEAR BE COMING!
- A GULLAH YEAR -

WRITTEN BY

Katharine Boling

ILLUSTRATED BY

Daniel Minter

Albert Whitman & Company
Morton Grove, Illinois

ABOUT THE GULLAH PEOPLE

Gullahs, or "Geechies," are African-Americans who live mainly in the southern "Lowcountry," the South Carolina and Georgia coasts and sea islands. They are descended from slaves brought from West Africa beginning as early as the seventeenth century.

From their experience at home in Africa, the Gullahs knew more about growing certain crops than their white masters did. The slaves helped to raise rice, cotton, and indigo, a plant grown for its deep blue dye. The Gullahs also knew how to cultivate foods originally from Africa: benne (sesame seeds), okra, black-eyed peas, peanuts, eggplant, sweet potatoes, and watermelon. Gullahs used their knowledge of African herbs to make folk medicines from native American plants.

Although most Gullahs became Christians, they kept their African heritage alive in their church services. Plantation "praise houses" rang with hand-clapping, foot-stomping, and singing. In spite of their new religion, many still looked to their "root doctors" for herbs and folk magic to cure sickness of the body and spirit.

In the Lowcountry, each plantation covered many acres, making the closest neighbors far away. During the hot summer months, most white masters and their families moved to a cooler place. Left behind to work, the Gullahs saw few people aside from each other and their black overseers. Even after they were freed from slavery, Gullahs often remained apart in their homes on the coastal islands. Thus, they developed speech unlike that of those African-Americans who lived in other places and heard more English. Their language became a blend of English and African pronunciation, grammar, and vocabulary. It is hard for outsiders to understand, especially when spoken quickly.

Native storytelling brings out the real charm of the Gullah language. Their folk tales, like "Br'er Rabbit," show wisdom and humor. Gullah folklore and language have also influenced the speech and traditions of whites growing up in this region. In addition, Gullahs are known for their music and dancing, cooking and craftsmanship. Their baskets made of sweet grass and pine straw and their colorful quilts show how everyday things can be beautiful objects made with great art.

The Gullahs have used their unique language, religion, and tradition to keep them together as a people. Close to the earth, their lifestyle is simple, but rich in heritage. Mindful of the past, they find joy in present things like the rhythm of the changing seasons.

January

In January month,
the sky the color of first dark
and the trees all nakedy in the wood.
Deer cock 'e head for listen
for the chop-tongue hound,
and bittle berry scarceful.

FEBRUARY

In February month,
ground mole deep for hide
and gray squirrel high for hide.
The God water slide down
puntop you back and down you neck,
and everything be cold.

MARCH

In March month,
the wind crack 'e breath and howl
like 'e be bex,
and the 'oman hang 'e shimmies on the line,
where them blow and blow 'til 'e come for get 'um,
and leave the door wide.

APRIL

In April month, praise God,
in April month, the jaybird cock 'e head,
and the yellow-bellied cooter start
for stir in the mud.
The first green let we know
the other green coming fast.

MAY

In May month,
first dark start to come slow.
When the sun for lean,
us got crickets in the box,
catfish on the line,
and hush puppies frying in the pan.

June

In June month,
every gal child take off 'e shoes
when 'e get off the yellow big bus.
'E start for dance and turn
and jump like rabbit and squirrel, all two,
but 'e play possum when Mama call.

JULY

July be sunhot month.
Gray moss full with chiggers,
and if them don't get you,
the gallon nippers will!
Dewberries hang with the stickers,
and huckleberries blue up you hands.

AUGUST

August month like yesterday dinner.
For truth, us think us through with 'um,
but 'e stick around
and dew the grass and mold the corn
and heavy the air so much
the lightning bugs be panting.

SEPTEMBER

In September month,
the gal child put back on 'e shoes
and wait for the yellow big bus
with new ribbons in 'e hair.
Now, the ground be swelling with pinders,
and Mama put yellow yam taters puntop the stove.

October

October be blue-sky and yellow-leaf month
when the red fox swish 'e tail
and the dusty-eyed coon go wading.
Us smell the fat lightwood kindling.
Soon us hear the hooty owl calling,
and us close the door.

November

In November month,
bobwhite rustle 'e feathers
puntop the brown stubble,
and the hickory nuts fall
next the crackly dry leaves.
Bobcat yellow 'e eyes when middlenight come.

DECEMBER

In December month,
daybreak poke slow,
and first dark come soon.
There be cake sugar puntop the corn rows
and fat meat to flavor you mouth.
"Christmas gift! Christmas gift!"

New Year

Now the sky the color of first dark.
"Bittle poor *that* day,
rest of the year be rich."
So us stir up the hopping John.
New Year be coming!

Hopping John

1 cup dried black-eyed peas
5 cups water
1 cracked ham or beef bone
1 onion, chopped
1 clove garlic, minced
2 tbs. butter
1 cup rice
2 tsp. salt
1 bay leaf
  a little thyme
  black pepper
  Tabasco sauce to taste

Wash and pick over peas thoroughly. Cover with 5 cups of water and soak for four hours. Remove the peas, and bring the water to a boil. Add peas, bone, and 1 tsp. of the salt. Let simmer for 45 minutes. Peas should be tender, and at least 2 1/2 cups of water should remain. If not, add water. Remove bone. Sauté onions and garlic in butter and add them to the pot along with rice, seasonings, and the remaining tsp. of salt, if desired. Stir, cover, and bring to a simmer for 20 minutes. Let stand covered for 10-15 minutes. Remove bay leaf. Serve with cooked greens and cornbread. Serves four.

GLOSSARY

All two — both.

Berry — very.

Bex — make angry, vexed.

Bittle — food, victual.

Bobwhite — game bird that calls "bobwhite, bobwhite."

Cake sugar — sugar. The cornstalks dusted with snow look
     like they've been dusted with sugar.

Chiggers — red bugs.

Chop-tongue hound — a hound that makes short yelps
     rather than baying.

"Christmas Gift!" — greeting on Christmas morning.

Coon — raccoon.

Cooter — terrapin, a kind of turtle.

Crack 'e breath — open his mouth.

Dewberries — blackberries.

'E — he, she, it, his, her, its.

Fat lightwood — pine heavy with resin, good for starting fires.

First dark — twilight.

Gallon nippers — large mosquitoes.

God water — rain.

Hopping John — traditional New Year's Day dish of rice and peas, believed to bring prosperity in the new year. It is considered "poor" since it is generally flavored with only a bone.

Huckleberries — wild blueberries.

Hush puppies — fried cornmeal dumplings sometimes thrown to the dogs to quiet them.

Jaybird — bluejay.

Middlenight — midnight.

'Oman — woman.

Pinders — goobers, peanuts.

Play possum — to pretend to be asleep or dead; in this case, to pretend not to hear.

Puntop — upon, on top of.

Shimmies — chemises; women's loose, shirtlike underwear.

Stickers — thorns.

Sun for lean — after noon, when the sun sinks lower.

'Um — him, her, it, them.

Yam taters — sweet potatoes.

To Hollins friends. — K. B.

To my mama, Mother Minter. — D. M.

Library of Congress Cataloging-in-Publication Data

Boling, Katharine.
New year be coming!: a Gullah year / by Katharine Boling;
illustrated by Daniel Minter.
p. cm.
Summary: Verses written in the Gullah dialect of the southeastern seacoast
describe the months of the year and activities that characterize each.
ISBN 0-8075-5590-8 (hardcover)
1. Months—Juvenile poetry. [1. Months.] I. Minter, Daniel, ill.
II. Title.
PM7875.G8 B65 2002   811'.6—dc21   2002001952

The illustrations are linoleum block prints.
The design is by Scott Piehl.